To Zachary —
Be good —
the Belsnickel's watching!

Chet Williamson

PENNSYLVANIA DUTCH

Night Before Christmas

Written by Chet Williamson
Illustrated by James Rice

PELICAN PUBLISHING COMPANY
Gretna 2001

Copyright © 2000
By Chet Williamson

Illustrations copyright © 2000
By James Rice

First printing, September 2000
Second printing, August 2001

To my Christmas angels:
Laurie, for suggesting this book and loving me;
Colin, for having become a man I can be proud of;
Mom, for being a bright example my whole life;
and Dad, who put all his love and craft into Christmas.

The author extends his thanks to Lloyd Arthur Eshbach, Dutchman
extraordinaire, for his linguistic assistance during the writing of this book.

Library of Congress Cataloging-in-Publication Data

Williamson, Chet.
  Pennsylvania Dutch Night before Christmas / written by Chet Williamson ; illustrated
by James Rice.
    p. cm.
  Summary: An adaptation of the famous poem about a Christmas Eve visitor, set in the
Pennsylvania Dutch country. Includes a pie recipe and information about the Belsnickel and
the Pennsylvania Dutch dialect.
  ISBN 1-56554-721-7 (alk. paper)
  1. Pennsylvania Dutch—Juvenile poetry. 2. Santa Claus—Juvenile poetry. 3.
Christmas—Juvenile poetry. 4. Children's poetry, American. [1. Pennsylvania
Dutch—Poetry. 2. Santa Claus—Poetry. 3. Christmas—Poetry. 4. Narrative poetry. 5.
American poetry.] I. Rice, James, 1934- ill. II. Moore, Clement Clarke, 1779-1863.
Night before Christmas. III. Title.

PS3573.I456238 P46 2000
811'.54—dc21

00-027748

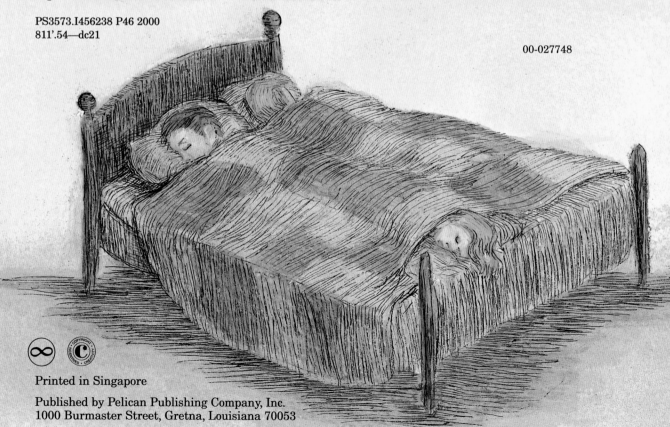

Printed in Singapore

Published by Pelican Publishing Company, Inc.
1000 Burmaster Street, Gretna, Louisiana 70053

PENNSYLVANIA DUTCH NIGHT BEFORE CHRISTMAS

It vas night before Christmas, und all over the farm,
Nothing vas *schusslich,** no cause for alarm.
The socks vere all hung by the chimney chust so,
Vith the hopes they get filled up from ankle to toe.

The *nixnootzes* schnoozing vithout any sound—
In their heads clear toy candies been dancing around.
And Mama and me, vell, ve outened the light,
Crawled under the covers, and schnuggled up tight.

**schusslich* (SHUS-lick)—moving around

Then from the awtside ve heard something fierce,
That made open our eyeballs and rattled our ears.
There vas crashing and banging and—could it be true?
Did our ears deceive us, or vas that a *moo*?

Then off to the vindow ve ran in the dark,
Kicked the dog accidental—he started to bark.
Ven ve looked through the vindow, coming in through the gate,
It vasn't *vun* moo-er ve saw—it vas *eight!*

Four cows and four steers—they vere harnessed somehow,
And vere dragging behind them an old-fashioned plow,
And there, chust behind it, as sour as a pickle,
Vas a fella ve knew had to be the Belsnickel!

He viggled that plow to keep going on course.
(I think he'd done better if he'd had a horse.)

So *dopplich** and slow those eight *dummers* did run,
And he growled and he grumbled and yelled at each vun:

*dopplich (DOPP-lick)—clumsy

"Now Jakie, now Becky! Now Rachel, Josiah!
On Menno, on Sarah! Esther! Obadiah!
And vatch vhere you're going! There's nothing unviser
Than stamping your hoofs into stray fertilizer!"

They got through the barnyard vithout any hitch,
And the Belsnickel grumbled and raised a big switch.
"Climb up on that roof now, and you make it schnappy—
You don't vant to make me no more unhappy!

"Macht auf on that trellis, then to the porch roof,
And don't get no ivy wines caught in your hoof!
I'll get awful *gristlich** if you make me fall,
So clamber up, clamber up, clamber up all!"

gristlich (GRIEST-lick)—grumpy; can also mean dirty or greasy

Like the chickens all look
    vhen to fly they're trying,
Or the mess kids are making vhen shoes they are tying,
So clumsy they climbed, up an inch vith each "Moo!"
But somehow they made it, and it vonders me, too!

And then in a tvinkle, ve heard on the roof
Each cow that vas *rutsching* 'round, stamping its hoof.
The cracks of the roof timbers filled all our ears,
'Cause it chust vasn't built for four cows and four steers!

By now all the kiddies had run in our room,
Frightened by all of those cracks and those booms.
To tell them vhat happened I vas going to begin,
Vhen, chumpin' chee zooey, the ceiling fell in!

Down came the Belsnickel, plop in our bed,
A few shingles making down, right on his head.
And vhen ve looked up through the hole in the ceiling,
It vas chust a little bit vorried ve're feeling.

For there overhead vas that eight head of cattle,
Still stomping so hard that it made the valls rattle.
Ve felt as if ve'd all been cursed and *verhexed,*
And that cows vould fall down into our bedroom next!

But they on the roof stayed, and I viped avay shweat,
Then looked at that scary old Belsnickel yet.

He had got to his feet and vas brushing his britches,
Holding his sack and using his switches.

He vas dressed all in black from his toes to his hat,
And he frowned and said, "Hey, vat are *you* looking at?
Ain't you never seen no Belsnickel before?"
Vell, I had, but the others had come through the *door!*

His beard vas all *strublich,* as vhite as snowfall,
And his belly so skinny, it nearly vas *all.*
(I couldn't help thinking that this crabby guy
Could use a few dumplings and shoo-fly pie.)

His eyes, they looked angry, but though they seemed vild,
Vhen he looked at the kiddies, he chust sorta smiled.
Then he viped it avay like he'd made a mistake.
(Or for him some *schnitz und knepp** Mama should make.)

**schnitz und knepp* (shnitz und nep)—dried apples and fluffy dough balls

Then he asked all the kiddies, "Haf you been bad or sveet?
If it's good that you've been, then I'll give you a treat.
But if you've been bad, then I'll varm your britches
Vith one of my special bad kiddy svitches!"

They said they'd been good, and vere telling the truth.
Still he glowered at Amos, he grimaced at Ruth.
He frowned down at Abner, who chust kinda grinned,
And the Belsnickel leaned down and tickled his chin.

"Ach, crabby I might seem, but don't you forget,
I ain't never had to spank vun kiddy yet.
It chust must be somesing arount in the air
Makes the kiddies act better at this time of year."

So his svitches he dropped and he opened his sack,
And he handed out oranges, yo-yos, and jacks,
A dolly for Ruth, and a vood horse for Amos.
Ve laughed as ve vatched him, and who could blame us?

And finally he gave to Abner a teddy,
Vith that final gift, to leave he vas ready.
But he said, as he crawled over shingles and sticks,
"I'll send over Stolzfus your broke roof to fix."

Then he chumped the hole through, up to his vaiting plow,
And he yelled to his livestock, "Get going—and now!
Down to the ground, and vithout no complaint,
Until ve get done and the houses all ain't!"

They sprung off the roof, to the yard vay below,
Vhere they got stuck in near forty inches of snow.
And that Belsnickel yelled, brushing snow off his head,
"Merry Christmas zu all, now chust go back to bed!"

THE BELSNICKEL

In Pennsylvania Dutch country, the Belsnickel often replaces Santa Claus. The Belsnickel is a crotchety old man, thin and bearded, wearing a long coat that comes down to his feet. In one hand he carries a bag of treats, and in the other he has switches, apparently to spank bad children (though there is no recorded occurrence of this *ever* happening).

Instead of coming down the chimney, the Belsnickel usually knocks on the door, and is admitted by the parents. The Belsnickel then grills the children on their behavior during the past year. Though he may frighten them with the switches, all get treats, and it is this Belsnickel who has been blended with the more widely known Santa Claus in this story.

PRONUNCIATION

Much of the charm of the Pennsylvania Dutch dialect (which should really be called Pennsylvania *German,* or *Deutsch*) is in the pronunciation of certain words. I have tried to indicate much of that in the text, such as replacing "ch" for "j" as in "chust so," and switching the "v" and "w" sounds so that "was" becomes "vas" and "ivy vines" becomes "wines."

One important aspect of the dialect is the "OW" sound, as used in the words "plow," "now," "out," and "ground." The actual vowel sound is a very flat and nasal "ah," as in the words "Pa" and "Ma." And "U" sounds should be pronounced as in "put."

In words like *"strublich,"* I suggest using the "ick" sound for beginning "Dutchies." But if you're up to the challenge, the more accurate pronunciation is a guttural "ch" sound, forcing the air up over the roof of the mouth.

I hope this will help you read the story aloud just as "Jakie Stolzfus" might have done it!

SHOO-FLY PIE

1 cup un-sulphured molasses
1 cup boiling water
1 teaspoon baking soda
3 cups sifted all-purpose flour
1 cup sugar
½ cup butter
9" unbaked pastry shell

Combine molasses, water, and baking soda; bring to a boil. Boil 1 minute, or until light in color. Sift together flour and sugar. Cut in butter with 2 knives or pastry blender, to a crumb consistency. Pour molasses mixture into pastry shell, cover with crumbs. Bake in hot oven (425° F) for 20 minutes. Reduce heat to 375° and bake another 20 minutes, or until crust is brown. Cool. The top of the pie should be a golden brown and a layer of jelly-like filling is between the crumbs and crust.